This Little Tiger book
belongs to:

_____

_____

_____

For our four little tigers, with love ~ M C B

*To my friends and family, also to two
little miracles, Jodie and Woody ~ C P*

LITTLE TIGER PRESS
1 The Coda Centre, 189 Munster Road, London SW6 6AW
www.littletiger.co.ukFirst published in Great Britain 2007
This edition published 2015

Text copyright © M Christina Butler 2007
Illustrations copyright © Caroline Pedler 2007
M Christina Butler and Caroline Pedler have asserted their rights to be
identified as the author and illustrator of this work under the Copyright,
Designs and Patents Act, 1988

A CIP catalogue record for this book is available from the British Library

All rights reserved • ISBN 978-1-84506-461-7

Printed in China • LTP/1900/1375/1115

2 4 6 8 10 9 7 5 3

Don't be Afraid, Little Ones

M Christina Butler

Caroline Pedler

LITTLE TIGER PRESS
London

Deep in the soft green shadows of the jungle Mother Tiger watched over her tiny cubs as they opened their eyes.

The cubs grew stronger
as the days passed by.
Little Kai learned how
to pounce . . .

and Amber
learned to make
surprise attacks!

At the end of each day the cubs
snuggled into the silky safety of
their mother's side and fell asleep
to the rumble of her purr.

Then one night Mother Tiger
went hunting. "Wait for me here,
my little ones," she said.
　　When she had gone the night
seemed bigger and darker, full
of strange noises.

The cubs waited and waited. "She'll be back soon," said Amber. But still Mother Tiger did not return.

"I do wish she'd come,"
whimpered Kai.
Amber stared anxiously
into the darkness. "Let's
go and find her," she said.

Through silver patterns of
moonlight the cubs padded
down the jungle pathway.
Dark shapes and silent
shadows followed
them through
the trees.

Then from
behind them
came a noise.

RUSTLE!

SWISH!

Amber gasped. "What's that?"
"I-I don't know," whispered
Kai. "Is it a crocodile?"

They stared into
the night, their
eyes open wide,
as the sound
came closer.

RUSTLE!

CRACKLE!

SWISH!

"Run!" growled Amber. "Run as fast
as you can!"
Crashing and bounding, faster
and faster, the cubs raced
through the grass.

"STOP!" cried Kai suddenly. In front of them the river swirled dark and deep. The cubs could go no further, and the noise was getting nearer!

With their ears flat and their
heads low, the cubs turned and
stood together.

"We're not afraid of you!" they
roared in their loudest, fiercest
voices. "Even if you are a crocodile!"

The grasses rippled and snapped,
then out stepped . . .

. . . Mother Tiger!

"We thought you'd left us!" Amber and Kai cried, leaping up to her. Mother Tiger nuzzled her cubs. "You knew I'd come back," she purred. "Follow me, little ones . . ."

Deep in the soft shadows of the jungle Mother Tiger and her cubs snuggled together.

"I'm not afraid of crocodiles anyway," Kai told his mother bravely. "Are you, Amber?"

But Amber was fast asleep.